Home Sweet Home

Written and illustrated by
Shoo Rayner

Ed had grey feathers, with six dark spots.
His beak was black and his legs were pink.

"Ed is just too grey," the birds said.

Ed was shy.
All day long, he hid in a hole in a tree.
"Ed is just too shy," the birds said.

When all the birds were asleep, Ed came out of his hole.

He cleared up the mess and then went back into his hole.

The birds didn't see Ed and soon they forgot about him.

One day, Ed flapped his wings and flew away.

"No one wants me here. I'll go and find a new home," he thought.

Ed flew across the world looking for a new home.

The desert was too hot.

The mountains were too high.

The city was too loud.

The sea was too wet.

But Ed liked the jungle.
The jungle birds were bright with colours.
Rose red.
Sunshine yellow.
Sky blue.
Jungle green.

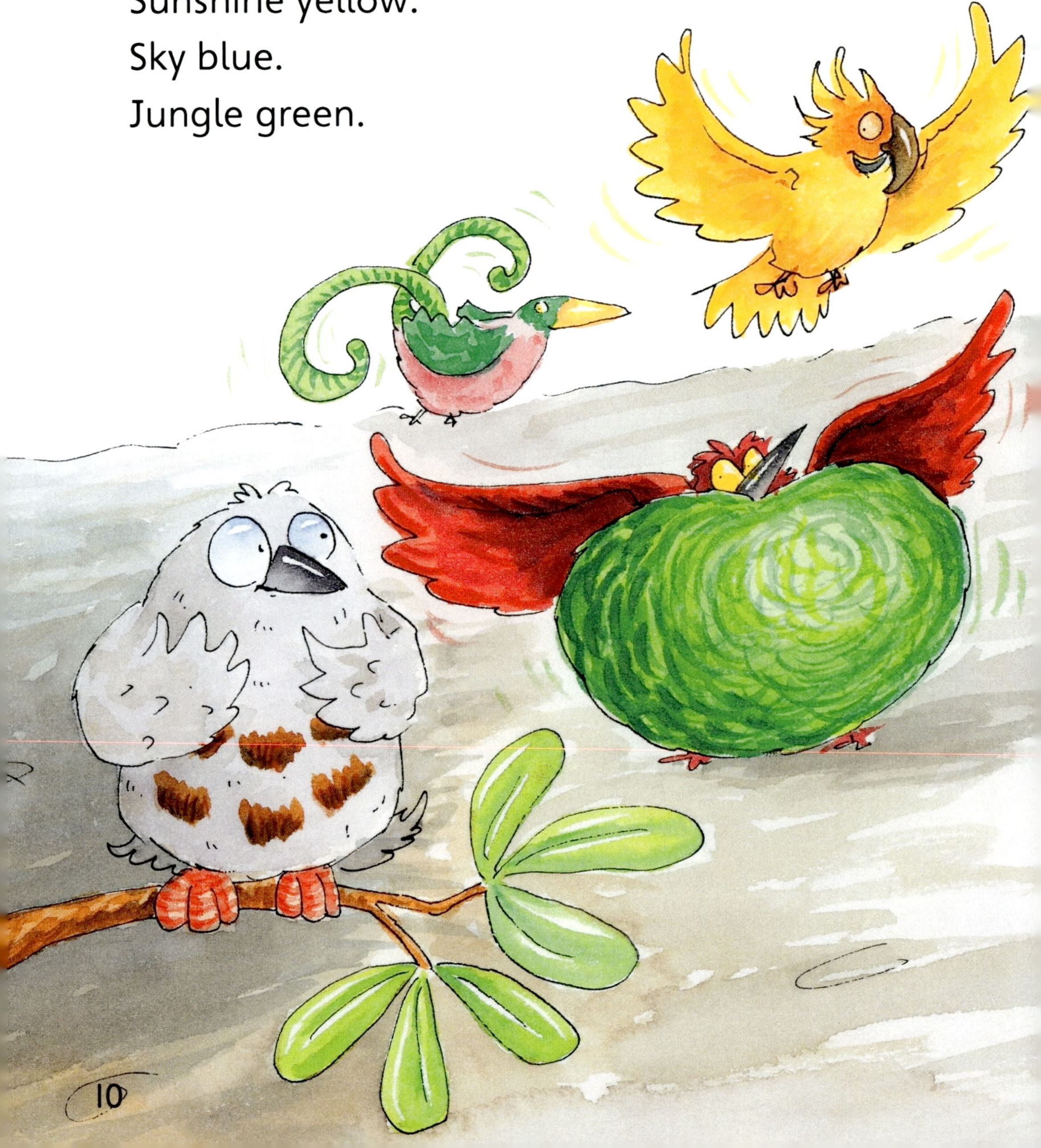

And when the jungle birds saw Ed,
their eyes popped out of their heads!

"You are just fabulous!" said the jungle birds.

"The spots on your feathers are as dark as chocolate.

Your beak is as black as night, and your legs are as pink as the setting Sun."

The jungle birds thought Ed was the most beautiful bird in the world!

They made him sit on a rock so that they could look at him all day.

But Ed was a shy bird. He didn't like being looked at.

One day, Ed flapped his wings and flew away. He went back to his hole in the tree.

The birds were pleased to see him.

"Hey, Ed!" they said. "It's good to see you. This place hasn't been the same without you!"

Ed smiled and began clearing up the mess.
"Home sweet home," thought Ed.